Wasim's
CHALLENGE

Chris Ashley

Illustrated by Kate Pankhurst

F
FRANCES LINCOLN
CHILDREN'S BOOKS

Chapter One

It was heaving outside the school gates, and the blue and silver coach was blocking the entrance, shuddering and pumping black fumes into the crowd.

Wasim the commando unswung his rucksack and sent it curling through the morning air. Everything he needed for survival in extreme conditions was in that bag. He was part of Special Forces on a jungle mission. Only the very best would make it, only the elite could survive, only. . .

Only Wasim's bag landed right on top of Donna Smith's bursting suitcase and sent a domino line of bags and cases skidding off the curb and under the chugging coach.

"Oy! Do you mind, Sonny Jim?" The coach driver, whose huge stomach stretched his purple blazer and whose bald head dripped with sweat, glared out of the darkness of the coach boot like a troll from under his bridge. With a mumbled "Soz!" Wasim had to stop being Special Forces and go back to being plain old Wasim Ahmed.

He retreated to the other side of the road where Mum, Dad and Shamaila were waiting to see him off, and watched his rucksack get bounced into the boot, feeling every bump and scrape as if it were happening to him. That rucksack was brand new and had been

waiting, ready for today, in his bedroom since his birthday. Now it was stuffed with brand new waterproof trousers, a brand new anorak, brand new thick socks and his brother's sleeping bag. The brand new walking boots were already on his feet, because it was here. The day. School Journey Day. *Challenge by Choice* Day!

O O O

Wasim watched Charles and Ellis testing out their boots by jumping on each other's toecaps, Dionne practising his rock climbing skills by getting halfway up a lamp post and Mr Abbot telling them all off and looking strange in ironed jeans and whiter-than-white new trainers.

Now Wasim had to make a quick decision. Should he go and join in with Charles and Ellis and make sure he was going to be counted as one of the lads this week? Or should he join David and Joshua who were helpfully handing the bags to the coach driver? Or should he try and be first on the coach and get one of the seats near the back that he'd just spotted? They had tables and lamps, just like footballers had on the coach driving them to a Wembley Cup Final.

Shamaila slid a little fist into his gloved hand.

Or should stay for a last few minutes with Mum and Dad?

Wasim felt a pang, a sort of dull thumping feeling. He'd never been away from them for even one night in his whole life and now he was going to be gone for four whole nights, and miles and miles away. Or wherever Wales and the CBC centre were.

"OK, everybody, last goodbyes and line up!"

Too late. Wasim was going to miss the tables, but the extra squeeze from Shamaila and the worried look from Mum meant that the pang felt worse than his coach worries.

In fact, he had a few pangs going on. From the top of his itching head all the way down. His head was itching because of his bobble hat. It was designed for the Arctic winter, but Wasim wasn't going to take it off.

His gloves had been presents with his rucksack, and at the school journey meeting last week Mr Abbot had said that you could never trust the weather. So Wasim was keeping them on too, even outside the school gates in the middle of June.

His next pang was in his chest and it was where his excitement and homesickness were meeting head-on.

And then there was his stomach.

That was the worst pang. He was hungry, and the packet of warm doughnuts that Donna's mum had bought from the shop over the road had made him long for food. It hurt, but Wasim wasn't going to give up.

"Come on, everyone, the mountains won't wait."

Mum pressed a carrier bag into his hand. "Packed lunch. Don't leave it on the bus. Some nan, a kebab, a banana, some crisps and a Mars bar, an orange and two cans of drink. . ."

Another pang – guilt! Mum had gone to all that trouble so that he wouldn't be hungry and would have a packed lunch as good as anybody else's, and he was tricking her.

Psst. Someone opened a can of coke and Wasim groaned. Now his throat began to feel cracked. He smelt the doughnuts again and tried to work it out: the time now was ten to nine in the morning, the sun went down at 9.13 in the evening... Only eight... nine... twelve and a bit hours to go. He wouldn't be eating or drinking for another twelve and a bit hours. *Twelve and a bit hours!*

But that was the *fast* – no food or drink between sunrise and sunset. That was Ramadan.

That was what Muslim grown-ups did, and this year that was what Wasim was going to do.

He would have gulped if it wasn't so painful inside his scratchy throat.

But then Wasim remembered the classes at the mosque and clever Faizhan who learned his pages from the Koran without seeming to look at it, and who complained and laughed when they had to spend so much time waiting for Wasim to catch up. And he remembered Faizhan smirking, his pretending-to-be-surprised look around their little madrasa teaching room when he found out that Wasim wasn't going to be fasting.

Well, Wasim *was* going to be fasting! The only difference was that nobody could know. Not even Mum and Dad.

Wasim gave a last wave outside the coach and made a head-down barge past the children fussing with overhead vents, putting hands up because of seat belts that wouldn't

click or cramming bags onto a luggage rack
that was already bursting.

He got to an empty footballers' table seat.
Phew! He had met the first challenge.

He was almost ready to take off his
bobble hat as he plonked his carrier bag of
food onto the shiny table under the lamp.

"All belts done up?" Mrs Scott was

working her way down the coach and checking as she asked. The coach driver was also working his own way down, busily closing the vents that the children had dared to open.

"Oy! No you don't. . . Them seats are out of use!" He enjoyed giving the bad news. Wasim had to squeeze out just in time to see Ellis get the last back row seat next to Charles. He lifted his bobble hat to have a panicked look round.

Nothing!

"Oh, Wasim. . . You again," Mrs Scott said. "Don't worry, you can sit next to Mr Bird and keep him company."

Next to the teacher? Not even a teacher, a *student* teacher! Wasim couldn't believe it . . . Mr Bird! *"Bird the Nerd,"* the Year Six kids called him.

Wasim felt all of his pangs come together, as he managed a last wave of his gloved hand, and caught a hopeful smile from his mum and a thumbs up from his dad.

There were massive cheers, waves and whistles, and before they'd even outrun Gemma's dog yapping its way alongside the coach, the lucky people on the back seat had started a shouting version of *She'll be Coming Round the Mountain.*

"Not singing, Wasim?" joked Mr Bird.

"Aye, aye yippee yippee aye," croaked Wasim.

Chapter Two

Year Fives went to the CBC centre every year.
CBC stood for Challenge by Choice and it
meant that you could choose how hard to
challenge yourself on lots of activities.
The centre was in Wales, near Mount
Snowdon, so they were going to be on the
coach for hours.

Mount Snowdon was the highest

mountain in the world. Well, that was what Charles reckoned.

Wasim didn't believe Charles, and Mrs Scott had told them that Snowdon was very small compared to Everest and K2 and lots of other mountains, but that it was still quite high. And they were going up it!

Charles said that they'd measured the other ones wrong and that Mount Snowdon was definitely the highest. But, as it had been Charles who had measured the hall and made Wasim announce in Achievers Assembly that it was 412 km long, Wasim believed Mrs Scott.

Whatever it was, it was still a long way away and in the sweltering coach even Wasim thought that it would be safe to take off his survival gear. His hat, gloves and anorak came off, and still the coach was steaming.

Up and down went Mrs Scott and Mr Abbot with the sick bucket, and when Donna was sick for the third time Mr Bird volunteered, and after that Wasim had to sit with the bucket and the smell at his feet.

"Gross, Waz," gagged Charles as he did one of his walks down to the front to ask if they were nearly there yet.

"It wasn't me," blustered Wasim, but Charles stroked an imaginary beard to show that he didn't believe him, and Wasim couldn't do anything about it.

At least the smell stopped him thinking about food for a few minutes!

○ ○ ○

But when the coach lumbered into a motorway service station and the bucket got taken away, Wasim started to dream of the kebab, the Mars and the coke cans bulging in his carrier bag. This was a challenge, a big challenge. Everybody else was going to be having their lunch now.

Luckily they were all too bothered with their own food to be interested in what Wasim was or was not eating. He carefully fiddled about in his bag, so that by the time the teachers started giving out fruit and drinks he had joined a toilet line, and then made for some swings where the early finishers were dashing.

Then it was back on the coach and another two hours of sweating, watching the sick bucket be re-filled, answering Bird the Nerd's questions about home and listening to him telling everyone about the places they were passing.

Eventually they came off the motorway, and instead of the crowded streets of houses and flats that they were used to around their school, they saw tiny white cottages and schools that were so small they could fit into their hall.

"We should play them at football," shouted Ellis.

"You'd still lose," Mr Abbot winked and Ellis went all red because he didn't know if it was a joke or not. They had lost every match last season, even though they'd had the Teamwork 10,000 coaches in.

In fact, sitting with Bird the Nerd wasn't too bad. Once they were off the motorway, he taught the people in the nearby seats to play Pub Cricket. You got a cricket point, a run, for every leg of the animal or person on the pub sign. If it didn't have any legs you were out, just like in cricket. By the end, everybody was crowding round wanting to play and getting told off for being out of their seats. And rather than having the worst seat, Wasim secretly thought that sitting with Bird the Nerd might have been the best spot, especially when they passed The George and Dragon and he scored six runs. Two for George and four for the dragon.

"Dragons have eight legs," he tried to claim, but six was still good. Anyway, it kept his mind off his tummy, which was now beginning to complain seriously. It kept rumbling loudly, and Wasim had gone from feeling a bit sick to it really hurting. The thirst was the worst thing, though. Breathing the boiling air on the coach into his sandpaper throat was agony, and he couldn't even manage a groan when the coach struggled up

one of a million hills and they passed a pub
called The Fox and Hounds. That meant that
Mrs Scott beat his George and Dragon,
because a fox had four legs and there must
have been hundreds of hounds in the picture.
Nobody cared, though, because now they
were nearly there!

"Hard luck, Wasim," laughed Mr Bird,
as they passed a brown road sign that
read "CBC Centre, One mile" and then

the same in Welsh.

The teacher put out a hand and Wasim shook it, and risked his throat by joining in the cheers as they passed all of the things they had been looking forward to: a climbing wall, a circular track with quad bikes parked and ready to go, a giant tree platform and, best of all – bristling way above the coach roof – the 'commando cord', a great zip wire stretching from a platform halfway up into space.

CBC. Challenge by Choice.

They were there!

Chapter Three

"OK, guys, are you happy to be here?"

"Yeah!" they shouted shyly.

"I said, Are You Happy To Be Here?"

"YEAH!" they hollered, Mr Bird the
loudest, which made everybody laugh.

The instructor moved his sunglasses up
onto his head, rolled his eyes and pretended
to be deafened, which got a better sort
of laugh.

"Right, guys." They all looked at each other. This was better than being called "boys and girls" or "children".

"Guys, my name is Mr Holden, but you can call me . . . Mr Holden." There were shrieks of laughter, especially from the girls.

"Nah, we're not at school now, so you can call me Dom." More secret smiles. No, they were not at school. This was a thousand trillion times better.

Mr Holden – Dom – was standing in front of an old mansion and the children were all in a straight line, with their rucksacks, cases and sleeping bags at their feet.

Dom jumped up onto a wall to show how fit he was and then started explaining.

"So, this is CBC – Challenge by Choice – Wales. There are some tough challenges here and we know you're really going to enjoy

them. You can challenge yourself by going high, or fast, or simply by passing the hill walk challenge. It's your choice. . . Get it? Challenge by Choice."

They all nodded. They got it.

"I'm doing it all," nudged Charles.

"Me too," said Wasim who had left Mr Bird and managed to get back with his mates.

"Is it dangerous, Mr . . . Dom?"

They all giggled. Trust Donna!

Dom put on a grim face. "That's a good question, sweetheart."

Donna beamed.

"Everything is dangerous here. Everything is safe here. It depends on whether you follow the rules. Rules are here for your safety so. . ."

And then Dom droned on about wearing helmets for all activities, tying long hair back, having asthma sprays with you at all times, being silent if an instructor whistled, staying in safety areas, not running between activities and not having food in the dorms.

"Rules are essential. If you break 'em . . . you're out. No questions!"

They quite agreed and they all exchanged nods, except for Dionne, who looked at the ground and smiled, because he knew that everyone was looking at him.

"So, you guys, it's time to unpack, get some tucker – that means food, guys!"

They all cheered.

"Evening activities – tomorrow, disco."
They all screamed.

"I hope you've all brought your best dresses . . . boys."

They all screamed again, this time with laughter.

"And tonight, an adventure game . . . IN THE WOODS."

Another massive cheer, arms gripped in excitement, and then they were off to the dorms.

○   ○   ○

They charged up the stairs and Wasim got there third. That was OK. He was still in with Ellis and Charles, but he also got the last top bunk in the bedroom, or 'dorm' as they called them at CBC.

"Top one, Waz. Get it?"

Charles had got one too, and Wasim did get it, but laughing wasn't something he could trust his tummy to do. The dorms were in another part of the huge house, and Wasim looked at the shiny wooden walls and remembered that really rich people had once lived here. But the rich people had probably had bulging bellies, not empty ones like Wasim's. And now Wasim's stomach hurt, really hurt. It was taking his breath away and making his legs feel tingly, like they were not his.

But at least he was in the right dorm. There would be laughs, but not too much trouble. Not like next door. Even though Dionne was with Wing Ho and Joshua, who were supposed to be good influences, there was no way Dionne could get through the night without getting in trouble.

O O O

There would have been a race downstairs to the dining room, but Mr Abbot was standing on the landing, so the brakes had to go on. Wasim wasn't in a rush anyway.

In fact, he was dreading dinner. His stomach was crying out for food, and when he saw the chips and pizza and the little orange juice containers he almost gave in.

"Wasim will fast next year," Dad had announced. The elders at the mosque had nodded. He wasn't ready yet. He wasn't ready to do one of the five most important things that a Muslim could do to show his faith.

They said it was because of the school journey. It would be too dangerous to try so many activities with no energy, especially at this time of year, when the sun was out for so long. Of course, if he were older, then there would be no question, but Wasim was not quite ready. He could fast next year. Faizhan had smirked again.

Wasim remembered that smirk and sat
with the rest of his school at the long table
stretching all the way down the old
Victorian hall.

The noise was deafening. There must
have been five other school parties there
and they didn't seem to have had the
behaviour and manners warnings that
Mr Abbot was shouting to remind
Wasim's class of.

The children had to take it in turns to
collect a tray and go up to the smiling servers
at the hatch. Wasim waited.

"OK, Charles, Wasim, Ellis, Sadie and
Donna, up you go. No pushing, and don't
forget knives and forks."

Charles and Ellis were up and off as if
it were the Olympic final, but Wasim took
his time and even let Donna and Sadie

in front of him, while his mind and stomach
raced.

And it *was* a race, a race against his
parched throat, and the smells that meant he
could almost taste the sizzling pizza and
home fried chips being piled onto plates,
until even Charles had to tell them to stop.

It was a race to ignore the creasing pain
shooting across his stomach, and to resist
getting the drink that would stop his tongue

feeling as if it had swollen up into a
monster-sized slug.

It could be easy. All he had to do was put
out his tray, say "thanks" and then tuck in.
The pain would all be gone and he'd be ready
to win this adventure game that Dom had
been going on about. Mmmm. . . Easy.

"Pizza, young man?"

The server was young and friendly, and
Wasim felt the hungry, tickly weakness in his

arms as they started to move his tray towards the pizza. He tried to think of show-off Faizhan and then he remembered the grown-ups.

"Not ready yet! Maybe next year. Not ready!"

How many times did he hear that?

Move to library books?

"Oh, Wasim's not quite ready!"

Move to the deep end?

"Oh, he's not quite ready."

Play for the school team?

Hardest shot in the school, but not quite ready!

"Got to go to the toilets, soz!"

And Wasim pushed his way back through "Oys" and "Watchits" and out of the canteen door, trying to think of anything but the empty plate he had left next to the hatch.

His stomach was in agony waiting behind

the locked toilet door, wondering what kind of children had scratched all of the names and jokes and who-loved-who into the wall. He stayed sitting on the closed seat until a charge past the door and a crash in the cubicle next to his told him that meal time was over.

It was agony. Ramadan was agony, but "not quite ready"? Wasim Ahmed threw back the door and headed back to the noise and the clatter of trays.

He *was* ready!

Chapter Four

Trying to get outside for the adventure game was madness. Children from different schools swarming through a door, throwing slippers and pumps into baskets and struggling into brand new wellies or blister-making new outdoor boots. Wasim put his full kit on, and only just made it to the meeting area in time to hear about the game.

Dom was there waiting. He wore his CBC

T-shirt with its arms cut off to look like a vest, shorts made out of jeans and climbing socks and boots. He had his sunglasses on his head and a whistle hanging from his neck. Along the line, boys started rolling up their sleeves into vests just to look the same, but Wasim – all ready for the mountain weather to close in – was boiling and his hat was itching again. At least the gnats swirling in clouds over every excited head wouldn't get him.

"OK, you guys, this is the game. . ."

"When are we going on the quad bikes?"

Trust Dionne.

"Maybe never, mate, if you can't shut up and do this activity." Dom was furious and Charles, just about to ask when they were going on the 'commando cord', snapped his hand down quickly.

The teachers, who had been last out, came and joined the group and Dom put his nice face back on. Mr Abbot and Mrs Scott had to go to a meeting, but Mr Bird would be staying, and they hoped that the children wouldn't let the school down and would do as Mr . . . Dom and Mr Bird told them.

"I've told them the rules, they'll be great," said Dom. "Right, guys, we split into teams. One team hides in the woods, and the idea is for the defenders to tag them before they can get back to this circle and pick up one of these tokens . . ." Dom pulled a coloured disk out of his rucksack, "without being tagged. Simple?"

"Yeah!"

"*Not* simple, guys. The defenders can only tag by touching the attacker on the arm with one of these." Dom suddenly flicked his

wrist and a bright purple frisbee curved
its way through the air towards Mr Bird.

Mr Bird, who couldn't have looked more
different from Dom – with his shirt tucked
into purple jogging bottoms – wasn't
expecting it. He had his hands in his pockets
and couldn't get them out in time. The
frisbee hit him on the chest, and his hands
jerked out of his pockets and knocked it up
into his glasses, which fell onto the floor next
to his sandals.

"Oh, sorry Sir. Thought you were up
for it," smiled Dom.

"Quite alright," gulped a breathless
Mr Bird, scrambling for his glasses on the
gravel. And he threw the frisbee back with
a wobbling flick that only made it halfway
back to the instructor.

A few whispers of "Bird the Nerd"

went down the line, and Wasim was sure that Mr Bird must have heard.

"OK. . . Teams! Half with me, half with Sir. Let's go!" Dom blew his whistle, jumped off the wall and a stampede raced to be in his team. Every single person, except Dionne, who never wanted to look like he was in a hurry. And Wasim, whose hat over his ears had meant that he didn't hear the instruction at first, and then because he sort of felt he should be in Mr Bird's team after the coach ride.

It would be hard being an elite commando in that team, but Wasim went and stood with him anyway. For the first time in his life, he didn't care if he won a game or not. He was really not feeling well.

"Aching, man." That was Charles's latest way to say how good something was. But

aching was the word for Wasim –
stomach-aching.

He was on the attacking team, and hiding
in the woods and creeping back to base
dressed in his commando clothes should have
been exactly what he'd been looking forward
to since Year Four. But he didn't feel like it
tonight, he definitely didn't feel like it.

Dom evened the teams up (groans from
everybody now on Bird the Nerd's side) and
they all charged for hiding places in the
woods. Wasim joined in with everyone,
crashing through the bushes and trees and
then, when the showing off stopped, he
felt part of the strange quiet that suddenly
fell over the woods as the city children
entered a new world. A world of gloomy
greenness, of crackling twigs and of a dark
smoky stink, as rotting leaves were woken up

by new boots.

But the woods could only take their shouts away for a split second. The silent moment past and then there were squeals of pleasure when a doe rabbit and her litter of white-tailed babies bolted for cover in front of them. And screams of real fright when an evening owl hooted its command over the tree tops.

The owl slowed the attacking team in its tracks, and heartbeats of fear, as well as excitement made them want to stick together as the trees got thicker and the light faded.

The first mention of a bogeyman brought more shrieks, and most of the team just made a half-hearted effort at getting behind a tree before starting the run back to the light and friends.

But Wasim saw a gap under the roots of

a massive tree that was lying on its side with scorch marks burned down its bark.

He managed to ignore the buzzings that could have been anything on the other side of his hat and only made a feeble effort at batting away the whine of a gnat which had found his hiding place. Then he curled up and waited. And when he found that it was helping his tummy, he curled up even tighter. He wasn't going to make a run for it.

This was just right.

○ ○ ○

Wasim didn't know how long he had been
there, but it wasn't long enough. Crashing
and shouting sounds made him start thinking
again. He thought he heard his name, but he
had found a comfortable position and he
didn't want to move.

But he couldn't stay there forever.
He didn't fancy being in the woods all night,
and he didn't like the buzzing. Charles had
said they had killer bees in Wales. He opened
an eye.

"Just Waz and Dionne left."

"Come on out. We know you're in
there. . ."

The crashing was Dionne. He was making
a run for it. And Dionne could shift!

"Come on, Waz. We're last." Dionne had

found him and was stretching a hand down
to pull him up.

Wasim took it slowly, weakly. The shouts
were getting nearer and Dionne was off
again, so Wasim started to move. He didn't
want to get left on his own. Nobody could
keep up with Dionne, but Wasim followed as
fast as his wobbly legs and knotted stomach
would let him. He swallowed something,
but he had no spit to get rid of it, and so
he had to trudge on.

"There they are. It's Dionne . . . and
Wasim. Charge!"

They'd been seen. Wasim tried to
go quicker but his legs didn't want to know.

The trees were thinner and it was a bit
lighter when Wasim felt something hit
his arm. "Got you, Waz! You're caught,
no getting out of it!"

The frisbee bounced on the hard
mud and did a twirl before settling down.
Wasim lumbered on.

"Oy, Waz! You're out! Got you. You've
got to take it . . . Waz! Sir?"

But Wasim wasn't interested. In the
gloom he saw Dionne streaking out from the
last of the trees and heading like a bullet for
the base. Then he saw a larger figure, Dom,
and a purple flash in the gloom.
The frisbee soared even faster
than Dionne, and then it
swerved upwards and
slammed into his ear.
He slowed for a
second – it must
have really
hurt –

but Dionne didn't show it. He streaked into the circle on the ground and picked up a disk and held it up like it was the World Cup.

"Doesn't count, Dom got you. The frisbee got you. You're a cheat, Dionne, so are you, Waz. . ."

"Err, no. Actually, well done, Dionne." It was Mr Bird. His voice quiet but firmer than when they mucked him about in class. He was talking to Dom. "I thought it had to hit his arm. Not his head!"

There was silence while the children waited for it to be sorted out. Then Dom spoke through a fixed grin.

"Did it miss his arm? Oh, then well done, mate. Your team gets a home run."

Cheers and boos, and Dionne finally rubbed his ear, but Wasim wasn't listening. He was still moving, he just had to curl up again. That was all he was bothered about.

Curl up, and it stopped hurting.

He lurched through the confusion of the attack and defence teams swapping over and carried on up to the main building.

O   O   O

Afterwards he remembered taking off his outside shoes and thinking that climbing up onto his bunk would be the last thing that he would ever do. And then he was in his curled-up position again, looking at the window and listening to the distant shouts and screams of people having fun.

Chapter Five

The strange thing about being so hungry –
and even worse, so thirsty – was that you
didn't feel like you were part of the world
anymore. The sounds and places and shapes
outside, they were nothing to do with him.

But whenever his eyes opened they took
in the window and a wriggly shape that
sometimes looked like a question mark and
sometimes a giant squiggle, like one of the

handwriting practice exercises he had to do every morning. It was getting clearer all the time, and Wasim forced his eyes to stay open. There was a ball above it now and Wasim realised that the handwriting shape must be a mountain or a hill. Mount Snowdon?

His eyes closed and he curled tighter as the tummy pain got worse.

And the ball? Now there was only half of it, deep red behind the squiggle.

The ball!

Wasim began to uncurl. It hurt, but he uncurled some more. The ball was the sun, and it was going. It was going fast.

Wasim risked the pain and twisted himself to the steps of the bunk. He didn't watch where his feet were going but just kept his eye on the glowing ball dropping behind the mountain. He looked at his watch – 8.55.

The sun didn't go down until 9.13.

But this was Wales, and it was going down behind the mountain earlier here. If it *was* Mount Snowdon, then you could keep Mount Everest and Ben-something in Scotland. Snowdon was the best and Wasim loved it, because it was swallowing the light like a huge greedy bird being fed a worm . . . swallowing, swallowing, swallowing. And then it had gobbled it all. Gone!

Today's fast could end!

Dad had told him that during Ramadan when he was a boy they used to hold up two pieces of cotton, one white and one black. If you couldn't tell the difference, then that meant that the sun had set.

But Wasim didn't need that. He had seen it go. The sun had disappeared behind the mountain and all that was left was a goodbye orange glow.

He half-jumped, half-fell onto the bunk underneath and fumbled for his bag.

Thirst . . . coke. . . That would need to be first. But the bag was tied and Wasim felt too weak to deal with knots. There was a sink just next to the bunk and he knocked a jar of toothbrushes onto the floor, turned on the tap and forced his mouth under it.

The water was warm and wasn't the

colour it should be, but it was wet. Wasim ignored how it hurt his throat at first, and he gulped and gulped until his tummy felt like a balloon.

Now the bag. Wasim wobbled his tummy round and ripped through the plastic below the knot. He fished inside. What first? He fumbled. He wanted something soft and chose the bread. Sitting cross-legged on the floor he remembered to murmer *"Ramadan Murbarak,"* a greeting for Mum, Dad, Shamaila and Atif, and then he stuffed

a whole nan and kebab into his mouth. He enjoyed the aching of his jaws as he chewed it

down, while his hands busily searched out the crisps and banana.

As he chewed he thought of his family at this special time for them all. Ramadan. It was the most holy of the Muslim months. It was a time for thinking how lucky you were not to be poor and starving. So during this month there would be no food or drink passing lips, from when the sun had risen in the morning until it had set at night. Dad had explained that people of their faith recognised this as the time when the angel Gabriel had shown the verses of the Koran to Muhammad, peace be upon him.

Wasim also remembered his class at the mosque, and the look from Faizhan when they had been reminded that the Koran had been split into thirty parts, one for each day, to make it easy for Muslims to make sure that they read it all through during the month. That was probably another of the things they thought that Wasim wouldn't be ready for.

Well, nothing had passed his lips from sunrise to sunset. It had been hard today. . . But he *had* been ready. And he was proud to have been such a good follower of his faith.

He would be tomorrow, too. Archery, orienteering and then the mountain hike.

Wasim stopped chewing. Tomorrow he would have to get through it all again, and he would need fuel in his body. He would have to eat the *suhoor,* the meal before the sun came up, while everyone else was sleeping in the dorm. What had he saved for when the sun rose at 3.30 a.m.? Wasim started taking the bits out of his bag and hiding them in the crack beside his mattress. It was only until dawn. Nobody would know.

There were shouts from downstairs and Wasim quickly climbed back up onto his bunk, rolled the carrier bag up with his United pyjamas and banged the pillow down just as the door burst open.

That must be Ellis, he thought. He was quicker up the stairs than even Charles.

Wasim turned. "Who won the—?"

But it wasn't Ellis.

Chapter Six

"That is about the most dangerous thing you could ever do, mate."

Wasim's glasses were on the floor next to the spilled toothbrushes, so he just stared.

"Leaving an activity without telling anybody. . . We didn't know if you were stuck in the woods, dead or alive. . ."

The others all piled in now, sweaty and dirty from the woods. After the fun of the game outside they now sat on their bunks, ready for Wasim's telling off.

"So, what did you think you were doing, fella?"

"Don't know. . ." Wasim managed to mumble.

"Not listening to the rules under that hat of yours?"

The instructor took a step into the room. He saw the toothbrushes on the floor and Charles's wet towel on the bunk.

"You'll need to get this dorm a bit tidier, guys, keep towels on the—"

Dom stopped. And all the eyes in the room followed his down to the floor, and to crumbs, a banana peel and a crisp packet. Then they all went back to him as he took his sunglasses right off and lifted the banana peel up with his pencil as if he was on *CSI* from TV.

"Food!" he sighed. "What happens if there is food in a dorm, guys?"

Ben chimed in first, "The dorm misses the next—" And then, too late, he realised what he had done. "Activity."

"Oh, well done Ben!" Charles exploded.

"Correct! I don't know what you guys would have had first tomorrow morning, but you'll be writing out our rules instead."

"Nice one, Ben."

Dom was on his way out. "And I wouldn't blame Ben. There is obviously somebody in here who does not know our rules. See you tomorrow, guys."

And he was gone, while the five puzzled and then angry faces on the bunks turned slowly towards Wasim.

○ ○ ○

"Sent to Coventry," they called it. No-one was allowed to speak to you, not even the kids from the other rooms, once word got round.

Wasim had gone and ruined it for his whole dorm. Eating upstairs! He'd broken one of the big rules and now the whole dorm had to miss the next activity, the climbing wall.

Charles and Ellis, who were supposed to be his best mates, were first.

"You always ruin it, Waz. Just cos you don't want to climb. You go and tell him it was you. . ."

Wasim tried. He had found Dom by the office but he was busy with the other instructors and a giant map.

"Excuse me. . ."

Dom wasn't interested.

"Danny's group, red walk, Sally's team are green, my lot blue. . ."

And Dom just stuck coloured drawing pins into the map until Wasim gave up and made the long, slow walk back upstairs.

Wasim had sat on his bunk, staring again, until Dom's footsteps and match-in-mouth whistle bounced around the corridor.

"Hand over the food, Waz!" Charles hissed.

And Wasim had fumbled for his bag, dragged it from under his pillow, climbed down the steps of his bunk and handed it to the silent Dom who was leaning against the door frame. Wasim couldn't see his eyes behind the sunglasses, but he could sense the coldness in them as he hung the carrier bag onto one outstretched finger.

"So can we do the activity now, Dom?"

Dom smiled beneath his sunglasses.

"What's the rule, guys?"

And he turned and was gone, whistling down the corridor.

"Night, Dom," came a shout from a girls' dorm.

"Night, sweethearts," came the reply, to shrieks and giggles.

But there were no laughs in Wasim's dorm.

"Cheers, Waz. . ."

"Thanks for ruining it, Wasim."

"Greedy Guts Waz. Now we don't get

to do anything."

Wasim hadn't said anything as they all decided not to talk to him.

He just sat on his bunk and was relieved when Mr Abbot popped his head in and said "Lights out." Then he didn't have to see anybody.

The silence had lasted all night. No laughs for Wasim, no jumping from bed to bed, no-one asking him for a ghost story. And the worst of it was that they were right.

He *had* eaten in the dorm and he *had* been stupid enough to leave the signs of it all over the floor.

Chapter Seven

Tuesday, and the silence was worse than ever.

While everybody else scrambled for the door and the first activity, the Room Five boys sat glaring at Wasim as the dreaded crate – full of exercise books for their diaries, paper, pencils and "extra work" – was pulled out from its corner next to the sweet machine. The glares got worse as they took *Comprehension Plus* out instead of putting climbing boots on.

Dom came and went. His whistle seemed to get even more cheerful as he saw the seven of them (Dionne had joined them for wearing his wellingtons on the bed) start work.

Dom's whistle stopped when Mr Abbot rescued them.

"OK. As it was the first time and we know who was doing the eating, the rest of you can go."

"Yessss," they whisper-cheered.

"Wasim, we are guests here and you broke a very important rule. I hope you've learned a lesson."

So Wasim was on his own with Dom, who was furious that the others had got off so lightly. And Dom started his tuneless whistle again as he yanked open the door to the sweet machine and, without taking

his sunglassed eyes from Wasim, ripped open
a box of salt and vinegar crisps and lined
them up behind their springs in a neat row.

Next it was pastilles, and then cheese and
onion crisps. Then his mobile phone rang
from its cowboy holster on his belt.

"Hi mate. . . Yeah, yeah. This afternoon?
My lot will be blue team, St Marie's tomorrow
will be green and St Thomas's red. . . I'll
check. . . It's in the office. Give me a minute."

And he made for the door, his pointing
finger ordering Wasim to get his work done.

Wasim had done his best with *Comprehension Plus*. He didn't understand the writing he was supposed to answer questions about, but the teachers from his school were outside and he wasn't going to ask Dom for help. They probably wouldn't mark it anyway, so Wasim just copied chunks of the writing out and waited for the hour to be up and for the rest of them to come back for a drinks break.

Eventually, the clock above the great old fireplace ticked the hour away and clattering boots, shouts and a crowd racing for plastic cups and jugs of orange squash banged through the door and brought the old building back to life.

"OK, everybody. Five minutes for a drink, toilets and then back outside."

Wasim carried on writing. He couldn't

have a drink and nobody was speaking to him anyway.

Finally Mrs Scott came over. "Wasim, you can stop now. Get your outdoor things and join in."

Wasim snapped his books shut, did his fastest not-running-walk to the crate, and threw his work in before anybody could think of checking that he hadn't done it properly. He threw a spare cagoule on top to make doubly sure, and then raced upstairs for his commando gear.

He bounced back down the stairs, two at a time, ready to join the scrum at the door. What was coming up? Archery! But there wasn't a scrum. There was Year Five sitting neatly on the floor doing pretend gasps, Mr Abbot and Mrs Scott looking worried and Dom standing by the open glass door of the sweet machine.

"Does anybody know anything about a box of Mars bars? No? Well, was filling this machine up and got called away for a minute and – hey presto, guys – no box of Mars bars when I got back."

That was when Ben came down from Dormitory Five.

"Wasim's been eating in the dorm again. I found this under his bed."

There was a real gasp from Donna and then lots of pretend ones, as all heads turned to Wasim and then back to Ben to watch him step over the three lines of children and then hesitate while he decided whether to hand the Mars bar he was holding to Mr Abbot or to Dom.

Chapter Eight

"Wasim, Wasim, Wasim…"

"It wasn't me." Wasim's eyes went from the phone to the floor, and then up to the Mars wrapper. Ben had chosen to give it to Dom.

"Well, it must have been, fella. You've already handed over one bag full of food, you're the only kid here who eats in our dorms and my people tell me that you didn't

touch your breakfast." Dom looked at
Mr Abbot then, as if that proved it.

Mr Abbot shook his head again,
obviously surprised and Dom sprang off
the desk, towering over Wasim. "Wassup?
Don't you like *our* food, fella?"

Wasim sat up. There was something about
the way Dom had said "our" that brought
Mr Abbot to life. He ignored Dom and
spoke straight to Mr Snow, the
centre manager.

"Right, well we will pay for the Mars box
and I'll talk to this young man again later."
Mr Abbot moved himself between Dom and
Wasim and spoke in his quiet-but-meaning-
business voice.

"We've never known Wasim to tell a lie.
Getting in trouble, yes. Doing silly things,
very silly things, yes. But not lies. We'll see

if anything turns up today before we take any . . . err . . . drastic decisions."

"Well, the boy's already admitted to eating in the—"

Mr Abbot cut him off and took charge.

"Like I said, we'll pay for the Mars bars and Wasim and I will have a chat later."

Wasim found his eyes drifting to the phone again. A chat. It would be home for him, no matter what. If they thought he'd nicked the Mars bars, home in disgrace! If he told them why he had food in his room and why he could only eat after dark, home!

Ramadan or not, you can't do challenges without food.

○ ○ ○

The chat was going to wait. This afternoon

was the hike, and making sure everybody had their full waterproof kit and proper footwear took up all of Mr Abbot's time, especially when Donna's dorm all came down in their disco skirts and party shoes in case there wasn't a chance to get changed when they got back.

The hike was what the kit had been brought for, and what the children coming back to school always boasted about. The leaders took a group up into the mountains and they had to use a compass and the map to get back. The winning group each got a free CBC T-shirt, but if you got it wrong you froze to death and mountain wolves ate you. That was what Charles had told them all.

They were being split into three teams, one for each grown up from the school. Wasim hung back – nobody would want to be with him.

"Come on, partner. You look like a man who can read a map."

Mr Bird guided Wasim by the arm and put him with the group waiting for the girls to come back from their quick change. Nobody said anything about not wanting him, and they even forgot that he was supposed to be ignored. They were all too excited about the challenge, Charles's warnings about bears and Dionne explaining what he would do if they got chased by a yeti.

A whistle blew.

Dom waited for silence and then said he was sorry for the late start but he had had problems to deal with all morning. Wasim did his boots up again and felt the eyes on him.

"OK, guys. . ." And Dom explained the rules. Wasim tried to listen, but the pain had started in his tummy and packed lunches were being handed out for eating at "base camp".

Mr Bird let Dionne hold the map and Charles the compass, and the groups set off, chattering and skipping past the zip wire, the quads, the Challenge by Choice sign and over the road. Then they were onto a track and passing a footpath sign pointing up into the sunlight. And then the chattering slowed and they were really in the hills. The children fell into rhythm and they were marching.

"I have heard that it's been said . . .
Hup, two, three, four,
Kids pick noses in their beds. . ."

And even Wasim joined in with a smile.

"And I have heard that it is true . . .
Hup, two, three, four,
That teachers pick their noses too."

"Aching, eh Waz?"
Charles fell into step alongside him and Wasim's smile became a grin. He was back!

Chapter Nine

Dom led the way. It was fairly easy-going
at first, and brilliant! Marching songs,
rabbits that jumped out of their way,
a hawk hovering over its lunch and sheep
that seemed to own the mountains and
lolloped past with bad tempered *baas*.

Charles spotted the first yeti, but nobody
else saw it, even though the girls all screamed
and got told off by Dom. He was in a worse
mood than the sheep.

Then it was lunch at "base camp" and back to the bad times for Wasim. Base camp was a flat bit of land where ancient boulders had tumbled from the mountains towering above them and come to a permanent rest amongst purple heather, ferns and sheep dung. Wasim got to the biggest rock while bags of crisps were being thrown out to all the other children. Wasim wasn't interested in crisps and was pleased with his rock, but somebody ruined it.

"Throw us a Mars, Waz!"

And then everyone was looking at him.

"Not hungry, Wasim?" and even Mrs Scott who had snapped at the Mars bar joker seemed to be checking what he would eat. Wasim pressed his back into the cold stone and had to go through the act of looking inside the paper bag to see what the cooks

back at the centre were tempting him with.

And it *was* tempting. A cheese sandwich, penguin biscuit, blueberry muffin and a bottle of special Welsh Hills mountain water. Wasim's stomach had started complaining, but as usual it was the thirst that was getting to him.

It was hot under his waterproof, and as base camp had got nearer, the walk had got steeper and harder. The singing had stopped and the puffing had started and all of the others had been taking great drags out of their water bottles.

"Not eating anything, Wasim?"

"Miss, I feel a bit sick, Miss, I'm saving it." He did feel a bit sick and his head was dizzy. But he was still on guard enough to go for his old trick of changing the subject to divert a teacher's attention. "But Miss, someone's been ruining the rocks, Miss. Vandals, Miss" and he stood up to point to splashes of red, blue and green paint daubed at the bottom of his rock.

But Mrs Scott wasn't worried about paint on rocks, and she had to move quickly to shout Dionne down from the top of the green painted rock that he was balancing on, anyway.

Wasim watched her go and felt as if he *had* stolen the Mars box. At least he got to put his packed lunch back into his rucksack with no more questions asked.

The groups split up then. They would all
meet back at base camp in three hours, the
time it would take to follow Dom to the top
of Lion's Lair and then find their own way
back down. Wasim looked at his watch.

"Back here by five then, Wasim?" Mr Bird

was pulling on his rucksack and squinting through the sun at the climb ahead.

"Miss, yes Miss . . . Sir."

But Wasim wasn't checking his watch for a meeting time. He needed to work out how long it was before 8.55, the sun disappearing behind the lion's rocky mane and his chance to open the packed lunch and kill the pain in his tummy.

There was no singing now. This was a clamber, not a walk. You didn't need ropes, but it was hard and the only talk was about legs aching and how much longer there was to go.

Wasim didn't even join in with that. He just looked at the next step, pulling himself up on the strong yellow grass that sometimes popped out from under the rocks. At least it wasn't so hot, and there were a few clouds skidding across the sun that had been parching his throat lower down the hill.

But it was hurting. His thighs were burning like everybody else's, and he had cut his hand on a piece of sharp grass that had saved him from falling as he balanced along the footpath – now just a narrow slither between the mighty boulders that kept going up and up.

"I told you this was bigger than Everest." Even Charles, who could run for every second of a football match without a drop of sweat, was panting and gasping for breath. The line had stretched out and Mr Bird was right at the back helping Daniel Timms who was gasping on his inhaler and Tia who had lost her welly and started to cry.

They rested after about half an hour and Wasim managed to find a way of sitting that

helped his tummy, as curling up had
last night.

"OK, guys. . ." Dom wasn't out of breath
at all and was standing on a rock waiting for
Mr Bird and Daniel to lumber into the
clearing.

"Right. This is Lion's Lair. We're about
a hundred metres from the top but I want
you to appreciate this view."

So they all had to stand up and look out
into the blue.

"Down there, that's the Challenge by
Choice Centre."

"Wow!" they exclaimed. It looked like a
lego house, and a white van going through
the entrance looked like a toy one.

"Then over there, you can just about see
into England. Up there would be Liverpool,
and over there Chester, and on a really clear

day you could see Manchester. And over there, that nothingness, that's ocean. Well, the sea, anyway.

"OK, ten more minutes upwards and we're there."

That ten minutes was done in silence and Wasim didn't know how he did it. He had seen two blurred centres when they had looked down, and wiping his glasses hadn't helped. His legs were hurting too much to be like jelly. But they were buzzing, and they certainly didn't feel like they were his.

Sleep. Just lie down and have a sleep, his body seemed to be saying. But no. He kept going, the pain from scrabbling on bleeding hands up the spiky stone path keeping his mind away from his hunger and thirst.

And then . . . they were there!

They were at the top, on the lion's back, and the little ridge ahead was like its mane. It didn't really look anything like a lion up here. But even feeling as he did, Wasim joined in the excitement of looking out over the whole world and having his breath taken by the wind.

"You OK, Sir?" Dom nodded to Mr Bird.
"It's easy enough coming down, they'll enjoy
it. Just stick to the path, it's only about forty
minutes down. See you then.

"Be good, guys," he shouted. "I'll save
you some tea." And there were some sighs
at being left with Bird the Nerd and
Mrs Scott, but he was gone, leaping down
the path with his hands in his pockets and
his whistle so tuneless that even the wind
got fed up and just took it away.

○ ○ ○

"OK then, guys . . . umm boys and
girls. . . Who wants the map?" Mr Bird
sounded enthusiastic, and snatching hands
soon had the map in its plastic case with the
compass attached.

"It's this way," shouted Dionne and they all set off after him.

"Stop, stop, stop." It was Mrs Scott. "First of all, let's make sure we can find where we are, just like we practised at school."

They put the map on the floor and crowded round it. Fingers prodded all over but Wasim couldn't make out anything apart from big brown swirls, patches of green and red squiggles coming nearer and then fading away. He was seriously unwell.

"We're here, Miss." It was Charles.

"Good try, Charles, but that's the middle of Wrexham and we are up Lion's Back Mountain."

Wasim took a step back and sat down, waiting. He wasn't hot anymore and he untied his anorak and hunched against the mountain breeze that was sending the clouds above the Lion's Back into racing wisps, galloping in from where Dom had said the sea was.

In the end Mrs Scott had to find where they were and point to the path that they needed. Exactly opposite to the one Dionne had been leading them down.

"Coats on, everybody. It's not so hot now. Off we go."

Mr Bird was at the front and Mrs Scott at the back with Daniel and Donna.

Wasim was back with them when the gust hit. It blew off his bobble hat and had everyone screaming and scrabbling for their new CBC baseball caps and sunglasses.

"OK, OK, stick to the path," shouted Mr Bird.

Too late. The caps had cost £5.50 from the Centre shop and Junior S couldn't afford to lose that much of their pocket money to one gust of Welsh wind.

Mr Bird blew his whistle and, slowly, moaning at sheep dung stains and cracked lenses, the group strung itself along the path again.

"One, two, three, four, five, six, seven. . ."

"Eight," shouted Mrs Scott as Dionne leapt onto Charles from a huge boulder.

"Eight. Who is missing?"

Mrs Scott's voice had lost its school journey friendliness. "Hush. I said, who is missing?" She scrambled for her clipboard and started to bark names.

"Tony, Tia, Daniel, Donna . . . Donna?"

"It's Donna, Miss. A yeti got her!" There were screams as another gust of wind hit and nearly bowled them over. This one had stinging bites of water in it and the screams got louder.

Now Mrs Scott meant business and Wasim's stomach gave a different flip from his hunger pain. He had never seen a teacher like this – she was scared.

"Silence! Quiet!" She blew her whistle. "Absolute silence!

"Donna!"

They listened. Wind. A rush of cold rain. Nothing else.

"Donna!"

Nothing.

"Donna! Donna! DONNA!"

Then they heard it – a sob, and then another, above the sound of the next gust that came whooshing in.

"Stay!" Mr Bird had a sudden command

in his voice and strode from the path towards
the crying that was coming from near to
the top.

"Coming, Donna!" Everybody watched
as he scrambled upwards and out of sight
behind a wall. Not a brick wall, but a wall of
mist that the last wind blast had brought in
and not taken with it on its howling way over
the mountain.

Chapter Ten

"You silly, silly girl."

Donna just wailed.

"OK, OK. . ." Mrs Scott softened,
but shook her head in disbelief. Donna was
lying on top of Mr Bird's anorak and covered
by Mrs Scott's. Sticking out at the bottom
was a very swollen ankle and a pair of
pretend-diamond shoes. Donna's feet
were ready for the CBC disco.

"I forgot I had them on, Miss."

Mrs Scott shook her head again and
the two grown ups moved off into the mist.

"Don't move!" Mrs Scott said. But
nobody was moving. Nobody was even
talking. It was cold. It was wet. And it was
scary.

They came back with the plan.

Mr Bird would take the group down and
Mrs Scott would stay with Donna until help
came to carry her down.

"OK, gang, I'll do the map stuff now, it's

sort of an emerg— sort of a difficult time."

They zipped up coats and jammed hats onto heads as hard as they could. The rule was that they had to keep one hand for balance and one hand for the shoulder of the person in front. Wasim was last to line up.

The fog and rain had misted his glasses, but he couldn't see anyway and he didn't care. The sweat from his walk up in the sun had made his T-shirt wet, and now it was freezing cold. His stomach was doing somersaults and the path looked like a tightrope that he had to balance on. And his legs *weren't* his!

"Bye Donna, bye Miss," the children called.

Wasim leaned against the rock, staring at the wet greyness, at the red paint that meant the yobbos must have even been up here, and the green lichen that Mr Abbot had told them meant that the air was free from pollution.

"Come on, legs – work," he thought he said, but it wasn't English, it wasn't Urdu . . . it was just a gurgle. Wasim's body had run out of fuel and he finally gave in. He let himself fall and lie down.

"Just for a minute," he told himself, "just for a minute." But even for his minute, Wasim remembered not to let the cold drizzling rain into his mouth.

"Wasim is ready," he murmured and he curled up against the wind and cold at the bottom of his rock.

○ ○ ○

Mr Bird lifted him up to where Donna was lying. Wasim heard the grown ups say something about the worry of being away from home and in trouble, and too many sweets. And then there was a new plan. Wasim would stay with Mrs Scott and Donna while Mr Bird led the others down.

There was no talking, hands were thrust onto the next person's shoulders. And the rescue group set off.

"Bye Miss, bye Donna, bye Wasim."

"Don't worry about the Mars bars, Wasim."

But Wasim wasn't. In fact he wished he could be sent home now. And as he shivered under the rock, he thought of Dad's warm car and Mum's cuddle and the cosiness of his own bed. Well, Wasim decided, as soon as Mr Bird came back, Mr Abbot could have his talk and then he could be sent home.

Wasim stayed curled up, shivering and

imagining he was in his own bed, until a really bad blast of wind hit him and he woke up. Then he heard Donna in Mrs Scott's coat chattering away about her dog and her sister and her mum. Mrs Scott gave him a kind smile and stroked his head just like Mum did. She was kind, Mrs Scott. And she was cold.

"You can have my coat, Miss," said Wasim, when another really cold gust of wind and rain burst in from the fog and sent the chill through to their bones.

Wasim tried to move his arms, but the teacher wouldn't let him.

"They won't be long now."

But they were.

"How long have they been?"

"Oh, not long!" sparkled Mrs Scott, looking at her watch on her shivering arm. But she mumbled something else and, as he tried to sit up Wasim could see that her face wasn't sparkling.

"Come on, come on," her lips seemed to be saying.

Wasim huddled up again and said his own "come on," as he tried to curl tighter and tighter. What if they weren't coming back? What if there really were yetis or wolves. He didn't think he could run very fast, and he'd have to rescue Mrs Scott and Donna, anyway.

He pulled his hat more firmly over his ears and heard something – clumping and shouts.

"Hello! Hello!"

"Oh, thank goodness. Here they are, at last!" Mrs Scott's voice was shaking.

"Hello, hello. We're over here! Thank goodness you've. . ."

Charles was in front, then Dionne, Ben, Wing Ho, Tia, Daniel and then Mr Bird. And that was it.

"But. . .?" was all Mrs Scott could say.

Mr Bird was out of breath and his voice was shaky now, too. "We couldn't see anything and there was a big drop just down the last path we took. I couldn't risk it with the kids."

Nobody said anything. The children were absolutely silent – the first ever time for Junior S.

Mrs Scott took charge and pretended to be bright and cheerful.

"My, my, what an adventure, boys and girls. Plenty for our diaries when we get back."

"*If* we get back," mumbled Daniel, but Miss ignored him and the two grown ups stepped into the mist and murmured urgently.

"OK, OK, boys and girls. We're a bit lost, and with the weather like this we think the best thing to do is to wait here for the people at the centre to come and get us. They won't be long now, the other groups will have been back long ago."

"Why don't you ring 'em up?" asked Dionne.

"Good idea, but no signal. But. . ." Then Mr Bird got his whistle and gave it to Dionne.

"You've got lots of puff. Take it in turns – three short blasts, three long ones and then another three short ones. SOS."

So they all took it in turns blasting the whistle into the drizzly clouds.

"It won't be long now. We're in a cloud here. It will soon clear and someone will be up to get us."

They were in a circle on the path, sitting on their bags and sheltered from the rain by Wasim's rock.

"What if it gets dark? Then we'll be here all night. We'll freeze and our toes and fingers will drop off and. . ."

Mrs Scott glared at Charles and he stopped but she couldn't stop the sobbing noise coming from Donna.

"Mr Bird, what time does it get dark, just in case we . . . umm . . . have to have our adventure for a bit longer?"

"8.55," blurted Wasim and everybody looked at him.

"We really have got to get down from here," Mrs Scott mumbled, as much to herself as to Mr Bird.

They huddled more closely together. Donna got put in the middle of the circle while Tia took her turn to do the SOS blasts.

"I know, I've got some wine gums we could all share," said Mr Bird, "we'll need some energy to keep warm. Anybody else got anything we could share?"

"I have," mumbled Wasim and sat up and tugged at his rucksack.

"Ooh nice one, Waz, I love Mars bars."

"It's not Mars." Wasim pulled his rucksack away from the blue bit of his rock and got hugs from everyone as Mrs Scott shared out the sandwiches, crisps, muffin and gave everyone one sip of drink.

"But you haven't eaten anything, Wasim."

But Wasim wasn't listening, and he wasn't finding ways of avoiding eating. He was back at his rock, staring. Staring, and thinking back into the warm of the CBC Centre.

"Mmmiss, Mr Bird, Mmmiss. . ."

Words wouldn't come quickly enough.

"Miss," Wasim tugged at Mr Bird's arms and pointed at the rock. "Miss, Sir . . . red…"

"Yes, I know, Wasim, you showed me before." But Wasim wasn't waiting. His excitement had given him a supply of strength from somewhere and he was shuffling down the path as quickly as the mist would let him.

He got to the boulder just as a panting Mr Bird caught up with him.

"Wasim, be careful – there are huge drops and. . ."

"Red . . . red paint. . . Dom said it . . . 'My lot, blue team, St Marie's tomorrow green and St Thomas's red. . .' It's a walk. . . It's a. . ."

Mr Bird suddenly let out a huge "Aha" sound. "Mr Ahmed, you are the man!"

And then they were back at the circle and Wasim's hands stung as everybody, including Mrs Scott, gave him high fives.

"Somebody quick—"

"Dionne," they all said.

"And how about you, Wasim? Are you OK for this?"

Wasim was up for anything. *Mr Ahmed,* he'd been called, *the man.*

Yeah, he was OK for this. He was ready! They were off! Wasim, Dionne and Bird

the— Mr Bird in front. They were hunting
red rocks, the red paint on rocks which
marked the way down the mountain. They
were rescuing Junior S.

"Red!!!" hollered Dionne.

"Dionne, you are the man," shouted
Wasim, and he overtook, ready to find the
next one.

Chapter Eleven

It looked like chaos at base camp, but it wasn't. Everybody knew what they were doing. They were moving quickly, but they were calm. There was a Land Rover with 'Mountain Rescue' written on it, an ambulance with its blue light swivelling, and there were serious men in orange cagoules with rucksacks, ropes and sticks.

Mr Abbot was talking to Mr Snow and

a policeman when he caught sight of their straggling line coming past the last rock with its ugly splash of red. Dionne and Wasim were at the front, and at the back, sweat pouring from his matted hair, was Mr Bird with Donna on his back.

"Wow! How did you. . .?"

But Mr Bird didn't have the breath to answer. He carried on walking until strong arms from the ambulance team took Donna and put her onto a stretcher.

"Oh, well done Richard," said Mr Abbot.

"Dom said you were on the blue walk." It was Mr Snow. A school emergency at his centre had left him seriously shaken.

And it was at that moment that a team of men in orange, followed by Dom, emerged from the boulder next to the biggest of all the boulders at base camp, one with a great blue splodge on it.

"Dom didn't say anything about any colours!" snapped a shivering Mrs Scott. Mr Snow and Mr Abbot turned slowly round and Dom looked at the ground rather than return the stares.

"Staff didn't know to follow the markings back down?"

"Err . . . well I had a lot on with the missing sweets and. . ." It just sounded silly and Dom stopped talking.

"And the 'lot on' included a footwear inspection, I suppose?"

"Err well. . ."

But Mr Snow had stalked off. Mrs Scott had a tin foil blanket given to her and all of the children were being given energy drinks.

"Is this the young man who collapsed up there?" asked the ambulance man.

"Yes," said Mrs Scott. "He's also the young man who got us down!"

"Well done, son," he said. "Drink this and then you're coming for a ride with us."

"I can't." Wasim pushed the orange liquid away.

"Come on, Wasim," said Mr Abbot, "even mountain men have to drink."

"I can't."

"Come on, Waz."

"It's Ramadan and Muslim men have to fast and. . ."

"Look up there, Wasim." It was Mr Bird and Wasim followed his pointing finger.

As fast as it had come in, the mist was rolling away and gradually a mighty lion with the strongest of backs and the fullest of manes was formed out of the rocks high above them. And behind it, blazing as if it felt no guilt about hiding all afternoon was the red ball of sun – going, going, going and . . . gone!

"*Ramadan Murbarak,*" croaked Wasim and then that orange was the best thing he had ever tasted.

"Thanks," he said.

"So," said Mr Bird, "fasting, eh?"

Wasim nodded.

"All day? Sun up 'til sunset?"

Wasim nodded again.

"No drink? No bread? No rice? No fruit?"

Wasim shook his head at each one.

"And. . ." Mr Bird saved the last one and hissed it straight at Dom.

"And definitely no Mars bars."

Dom tried to stare him out. But then he walked off.

"They said I wasn't ready," Wasim remembered explaining to someone, and then the dark sky, the glow around the lion's back and the grey rocks with their splashes of paint all span into one and he was spinning with them.

○ ○ ○

Wasim was back from the hospital by eleven and he wasn't surprised to see Dad's car outside the front entrance. He got out of the CBC minibus on strong legs and looked sadly up at the zip wire. The longest in Europe. Trust him to miss it!

So there was a cuddle from Mum and a proud hair ruffle from Dad, but then Dad forgot himself and it was a cuddle from him too.

"I think our son was worried that he would not be able to take part in all of the activities if it was known he was fasting.

But at this age in the life of a Muslim man"
– and Wasim glowed inside – "it would be
acceptable to drink, maybe, an energy drink
and still be following the spirit of Ramadan."

"Then Wasim would still be able to take
part in challenges?"

"Yes," agreed Dad. "We think he is
ready."

Wasim fought with his mouth to stop it

from smiling.

"Sir, Sir, guess what Dionne's done?"

A crowd had suddenly appeared in the corner of the games room, around a pillowcase that had obviously been in battle. Its corners were torn and its spongy filling was trailing all over the floor.

"Dionne!"

"I know," sighed Dionne, "*Comprehension Plus.*"

Mr Abbot almost smiled as he nodded to the crate.

Dionne did his don't-care-walk over to the sweet machine and pulled out the work crate.

"Sir?"

"Two pages, Dionne!"

"Sir!"

"Yes, Dionne?"

"Look!"

And they all got up and followed Dionne's pointing finger down to the bottom of the sweet machine and into the space where the crate had been. The space where there was a squashed exercise book and a flattened black shiny box with red squiggly writing on the front.

Dionne read the words out loud, "'Mars, vending pack, 24.' Not even opened. I knew Wasim didn't nick 'em, Sir. . ."

Mr Abbot smiled and looked straight at Wasim.

"So did I, Dionne, so did I. So who had just thrown all of that stuff into the crate like that?"

The Headteacher picked up the orange exercise book, turned it round and read the name.

There was a cough and Mr Abbot let out a sigh.

"Wasim, Wasim, Wasim."

O   O   O

Wasim gave Mum and Dad a last kiss and waved their car off into the darkness, and Dionne somehow managed to escape from *Comprehension Plus* to join in the goodbyes and the race upstairs before lights out.

"Ready for the zip wire tomorrow, Waz?" And Dionne banged on the girls' dorm door, made a ghost noise and dragged Wasim with him in the fastest corridor run ever.

Wasim made it to his dorm just as the screams had the stairs creaking and the teachers on their way up. He grinned.

" 'Course I'm ready!"

Also available:

Wasim the Wanderer
(selected for Boys into Books 5-11)

Wasim One Star
(A Scholastic Best Book of the Year)

Praise for other *Wasim* titles:

"A character that primary school
children and teachers will recognise
and respond to with pleasure."
The Guardian

CHRIS ASHLEY

Chris Ashley is a headteacher in the north of England. He loves school journeys and still goes to an outdoor pursuits centre every year with the Year Six children at his school.

They do all of the things that Wasim and his friends planned to do, and Chris gets just as excited as the children. He loves the quad bikes, and being in the fresh air, but what nobody knows is that he has a terrible fear of heights.

The very worst thing that he hears each year is when it is time to go on the highest zip wire in Europe. "Are you having a turn, Sir?" the instructors ask. "No!" he wants to scream, but he has to smile and nod, and then try not to let the children hear his knees banging together.

Also available from
Frances Lincoln Children's Books

Wasim the Wanderer

Chris Ashley
Illustrated by Kate Pankhurst

No one at school can score a goal like Wasim!
So he is trying out his football skills for
Teamwork 10,000 and that might just lead
to a trial with the Woodley Wanderers! But how
can he play his best football with Robert Bailey
lurking around every corner – and then
on the football pitch too?

Wasim One Star

Chris Ashley
Illustrated by Kate Pankhurst

Wasim wants to be a One-Star swimmer.
But when the day comes to take the plunge,
Wasim's up to his neck in trouble. When Wasim
gets ordered out of the pool for talking to the
new boy, Wayne, his chances of getting his One Star
vanish. Will Wasim be a star or must he wait
until next year for his chance to shine?